Hip, Hip, Hooray Day!

A Hip & Hop Story

BARNEY SALTZBERG

GULLIVER BOOKS
HARCOURT, INC.
San Diego   New York   London

www.harcourt.com

Gulliver Books is a trademark of Harcourt, Inc.,
registered in the United States of America and/or other jurisdictions.

Library of Congress Cataloging-in-Publication Data
Saltzberg, Barney.
Hip, Hip, hooray day!: a Hip & Hop story/Barney Saltzberg.
p.   cm.
"Gulliver Books."
Summary: Hop has trouble surprising Hip on her birthday.
[1. Birthdays—Fiction.   2. Hippopotamus—Fiction.
3. Best friends—Fiction.   4. Friendship—Fiction.]   I. Title.
PZ7.S1552Hk   2002
[E]—dc21   2001001384
ISBN 0-15-202495-6

First edition
A C E G H F D B

Manufactured in China

The illustrations in this book were done in pen-and-ink,
Dr. Martin's Watercolors, and Prisma colored pencils.
The display type was set in Boink.
The text type was set in Souvenir.
Color separations by Bright Arts Ltd., Hong Kong
Manufactured by South China Printing Company, Ltd., China
This book was printed on totally chlorine-free Nymolla Matte Art paper.
Production supervision by Sandra Grebenar and Ginger Boyer
Designed by Ivan Holmes

CHAPTER ONE

Hip couldn't wait. Her birthday was only a week away, and she knew exactly what she wanted. *More than anything else in the whole world, I wish I could go to the Royal Roller Rink and rent roller skates,* she thought.

Hip decided she needed a plan so Hop would know exactly what she wanted.

The next day on the way to the library, Hip told Hop she knew a shortcut.

"Why, what a surprise!" she said. "Wouldn't it be fun to rent roller skates someday *soon*? Like maybe a week from now? Possibly at noon?"

"We're supposed to be going to the library!" said Hop.
"It's nowhere near here."
"Oops!" said Hip. "My mistake!"

At the library, Hip only took out books about roller-skating. And for the rest of the week, she left hints about what she wanted for her birthday.

She drew pictures.

She trimmed the bushes.

She even walked as if she were skating.

By the end of the week, Hip was *sure* Hop had to know
how much she wanted to go to the Royal Roller Rink and
rent roller skates.

CHAPTER TWO

On the morning of Hip's birthday, Snooter and Peapod came over to help Hop.

"Hip's birthday is going to be perfect," Hop told them. "I got her the best present any friend could ever get. It's just what she wants!"

"Are you sure she doesn't know about her surprise party?" asked Snooter.

"All she knows is today is Hip, Hip, Hooray Day, and after that, *everything* will be a surprise!" said Hop.

"I love surprises!" said Peapod. "I think I'll plan a surprise party for *my* next birthday."

"Let's go over the plans one more time," Hop suggested. "At eleven thirty-five, I'll go get Hip and you two can start blowing up balloons.

"At eleven thirty-five and twenty seconds, I'll be at Hip's house and you two should *still* be blowing up balloons. At eleven thirty-nine, I'll give Hip her first present," said Hop.

"Are we still blowing up balloons?" Peapod interrupted.

"Yes!" said Snooter.

Just then someone knocked at the door.

"Yoo-hoo!" called Hip. "I'm ready for Hip, Hip, Hooray Day!"

"What are you doing *here*?" Hop called back. "I told you I'd come to *your* house!"

"I'm so *excited*," said Hip. "I couldn't wait any longer!"

"She's spoiling the plans!" Hop whispered to Snooter and
Peapod. "I haven't wrapped her last present yet!"

"Don't worry, I'll wrap it for you," said Peapod. "I'll do
something so special that *I'll* want to open it!"

"Just don't forget," said Hop. "We'll be back at noon, for
The Surprise!"

"We won't forget!" said Snooter and Peapod.

Hop put on his coat and scarf and slipped through the door. "Happy birthday," he said, handing Hip her first present.

"Hmmmm. I wonder what *this* could be?" she said.

But before she could open the envelope, the wind
snatched it away.

"I'll get it!" said Hip. *After all,* she thought, *it would be
awful to lose two tickets to the Royal Roller Rink!*

The two friends chased the envelope, but the wind blew it far away and finally out of sight.

"This is terrible," said Hip.

"That's okay," said Hop. "I can come over and sort your socks anyway."

"What do you mean?" asked Hip.

"I made you a coupon for me to come over to your house and sort your socks!" said Hop. "There's nothing better than starting off another year knowing where all your socks are!"

"Oh," said Hip. "I thought it was something else."

"Now, don't let this one blow away," Hop said as he handed Hip another envelope.

Oh, yea, we're going to the Royal Roller Rink after all, thought Hip. She hugged Hop. "I knew you'd get me just what I wanted!"

"And *I* knew you'd like a coupon for a tooth polish and floss," said Hop. "There's also nothing better than starting off another year with shiny clean teeth!"

"But it's my birthday!" Hip cried. "I wanted to start off another year having *fun*!"

"Hip, Hip, Hooray Day isn't over yet," said Hop. "I still have lots of fun planned for you."

"Well, it's over for me!" said Hip. "You obviously don't
know what fun is. I left hints all week. If you were really my
best friend, you would have known how I wanted to spend
my birthday!"

"Well, *you're* the one who came to my house this morning when you should have waited for me to pick you up. If I had given you your present inside, like I had planned, your coupon never would have blown away and we'd be at the fun part by now!" yelled Hop.

"Well, I'm not having fun right now," said Hip. "So I'm going home."

"But it's Hip, Hip, Hooray Day," said Hop. "And *you're* Hip!"

It was too late. Hip closed her front door.

"We didn't even get to sing 'Happy Birthday'!" Hop shouted.

CHAPTER THREE

I can't believe I had a fight with my best friend on her birthday," Hop said as he walked into his house.

"SURPRISE!" sang Snooter and Peapod.

Hop stomped right past his friends and into his room, slamming the door behind him.

"Well!" said Peapod. "*I'm* surprised!"

"Where's Hip?" Snooter called to Hop.

"She didn't like Hip, Hip, Hooray Day," said Hop. "She went home, and I don't even care!"

"That's not good," said Peapod.

"Let's go talk to Hip," said Snooter.

So Snooter and Peapod went to see Hip.

"What are you doing here?" asked Hip.

"It's your birthday!" said Snooter. "But you don't look like the happy hippo birthday girl to me. What's wrong?"

"I dropped hints all week, but my best friend still doesn't know what I want for my birthday," answered Hip.

"But the day isn't over!" said Snooter.

"Hop said the same thing," said Hip.

"Well, Hop has a really great surprise for you," said Peapod. "But we found out that it's hard to surprise somebody if she doesn't show up!"

"Come back to Hop's house," said Snooter. "We want to celebrate the day you were born!"

"And eat cake!" said Peapod.

"Well," Hip said slowly, "I wasn't looking forward to spending my birthday alone."

Hip banged on Hop's door. "Hey, Hop!" she called. "How about singing the birthday song with your friend who almost ruined Hip, Hip, Hooray Day?"

Hop opened his door and smiled. "There's nothing like a
good song to celebrate your birthday," he said.

Then he sat down at the piano.

Teek, teek, teek was the only sound that came out of the piano.

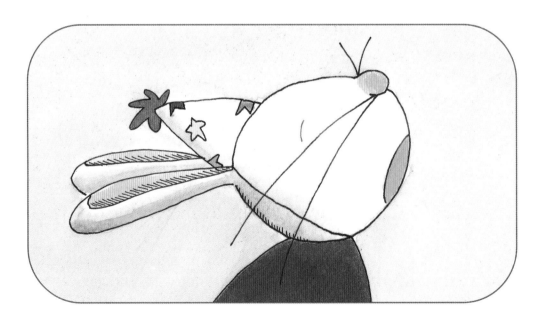

"That's not fair!" cried Hop. "Nothing is going right. I wanted your birthday to be so perfect! I planned everything, and *everything* has gone wrong!"

"I think your piano is just full!" said Peapod.

"Full of what?" asked Hip and Hop.

"Full of surprises!" said Peapod. "I told you I would find a special way to wrap your present for Hip!"

Hip opened the piano.

"Wow!" she said to Hop. "I didn't think you knew what I wanted for my birthday, and you found something even *better*!"

"Now you don't have to wait to go to the Royal Roller
Rink," said Snooter.
"You can skate anywhere!" said Peapod.

"There's nothing better than starting off another year
with your very own pair of roller skates," said Hop.

"Now *this* is what I call a birthday!" said Hip.

Hop smiled. "There's also nothing better than starting off another year rearranging your furniture!"